Dear Parents:

Congratulations! Your child is taking the first steps on an exciting journey. The destination? Independent reading!

STEP INTO READING® will help your child get there. The program offers five steps to reading success. Each step includes fun stories and colorful art or photographs. In addition to original fiction and books with favorite characters, there are Step into Reading Non-Fiction Readers, Phonics Readers and Boxed Sets, Sticker Readers, and Comic Readers—a complete literacy program with something to interest every child.

Learning to Read, Step by Step!

Ready to Read Preschool–Kindergarten
• big type and easy words • rhyme and rhythm • picture clues
For children who know the alphabet and are eager to begin reading.

Reading with Help Preschool–Grade 1
• basic vocabulary • short sentences • simple stories
For children who recognize familiar words and sound out new words with help.

Reading on Your Own Grades 1–3
• engaging characters • easy-to-follow plots • popular topics
For children who are ready to read on their own.

Reading Paragraphs Grades 2–3
• challenging vocabulary • short paragraphs • exciting stories
For newly independent readers who read simple sentences with confidence.

Ready for Chapters Grades 2–4
• chapters • longer paragraphs • full-color art
For children who want to take the plunge into chapter books but still like colorful pictures.

STEP INTO READING® is designed to give every child a successful reading experience. The grade levels are only guides; children will progress through the steps at their own speed, developing confidence in their reading.

Remember, a lifetime love of reading starts with a single step!

Step into Reading, Random House, and the Random House colophon are registered trademarks of Penguin Random House LLC.

Visit us on the Web!
StepIntoReading.com
rhcbooks.com

Educators and librarians, for a variety of teaching tools, visit us at RHTeachersLibrarians.com

ISBN 978-0-7364-4055-4 (trade) — ISBN 978-0-7364-8291-2 (lib. bdg.)
ISBN 978-0-7364-4056-1 (ebook)

Printed in the United States of America   10 9 8 7 6 5 4 3 2 1

STEP 2 INTO READING®

STEP 2 READING WITH HELP

DISNEY · PIXAR

TOY STORY 4

Ducky and Bunny Help Out!

story by Suzanne Francis

adapted by Lauren Clauss

illustrated by the Disney Storybook Art Team

Random House 🏠 New York

Bo Peep and Woody
help toys find kids.

Bo swings into action
with her sticky hand.

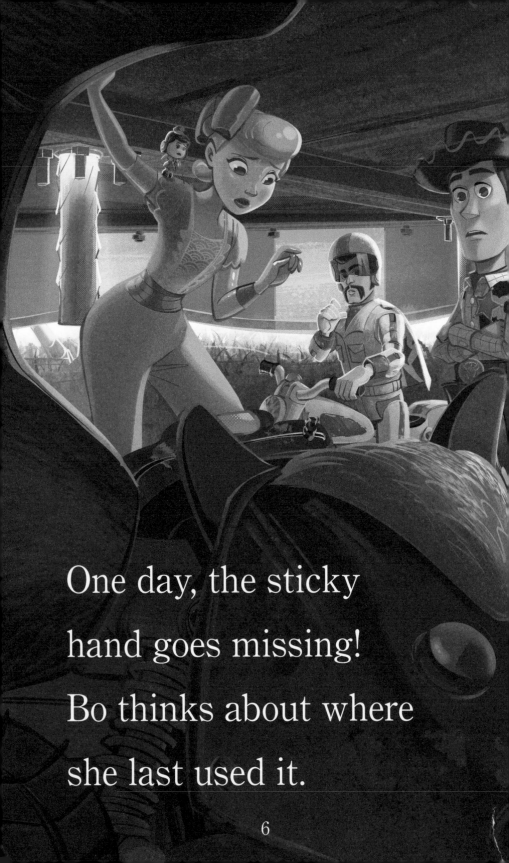

One day, the sticky
hand goes missing!
Bo thinks about where
she last used it.

It was at the Star
Adventurer booth!

Ducky and Bunny
know that booth.
They have a plan
to get the hand back.

First, the sheep will
drive the skunkmobile
through a crowd.

Ducky and Bunny will use a balloon to float over the booth.

Then they will fall
on the booth owner
and make him give
the hand back!
But Bo says no.

Instead, Ducky and Bunny
will trick the booth owner
into the fun house.

Then they will follow

him inside . . .

and through the
mirror maze . . .

and put him
in a trance!

Duke Caboom does not
think that will work.

Ducky and Bunny
have another plan.
They say it is
the perfect one.

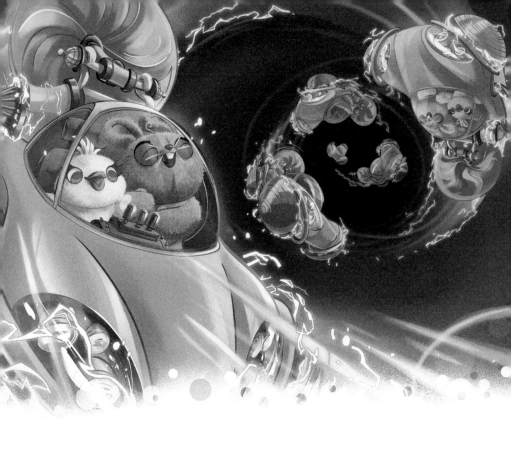

They will climb into
a time machine.
They will go back . . .

to the time of dinosaurs!

Officer Giggle says
they will not have
to go back in time.

The sticky hand is stuck
to Bunny's back!
She has cracked the case.

Bo is ready for her
next big adventure!